For Laura, Sylvie, and Paula.
Thank you for the remarkable adventure.
—L. M.

For Katie, Ben, and George.
—D. L.

SIMON & SCHUSTER BOOKS FOR YOUNG READERS
An imprint of Simon & Schuster Children's Publishing Division
1230 Avenue of the Americas, New York, New York 10020
Text copyright © 2019 by Lisa Mantchev
Illustrations copyright © 2019 by David Litchfield
All rights reserved, including the right of reproduction in whole or in part in any form.
SIMON & SCHUSTER BOOKS FOR YOUNG READERS is a trademark of Simon & Schuster, Inc.
For information about special discounts for bulk purchases, please contact Simon & Schuster Special Sales
at 1-866-506-1949 or business@simonandschuster.com.
The Simon & Schuster Speakers Bureau can bring authors to your live event. For more information or to book an event,
contact the Simon & Schuster Speakers Bureau at 1-866-248-3049 or visit our website at www.simonspeakers.com.
Book design by Chloë Foglia
The text for this book was set in Herschel and Golden Cockerel.
The illustrations for this book were rendered in mixed media and digitally.
Manufactured in China
0619 SCP
First Edition
2 4 6 8 10 9 7 5 3 1
CIP data for this book is available from the Library of Congress.
ISBN 9781481497176
ISBN 9781481497183 (eBook)

Remarkables

By Lisa Mantchev Illustrated by David Litchfield

A Paula Wiseman Book
Simon & Schuster Books for Young Readers
New York London Toronto Sydney New Delhi

The world is a remarkable place,

which means sometimes you go looking for a fish . . .

and meet a mermaid instead.

Some memories become the stories written on your heart.

Some stories become the dream written on your soul.

And sometimes the ending to one remarkable story . . .

. . . is the beginning of another.

Every day the remarkable world

gets a little bigger . . .

a little wider . . .

...a little brighter.

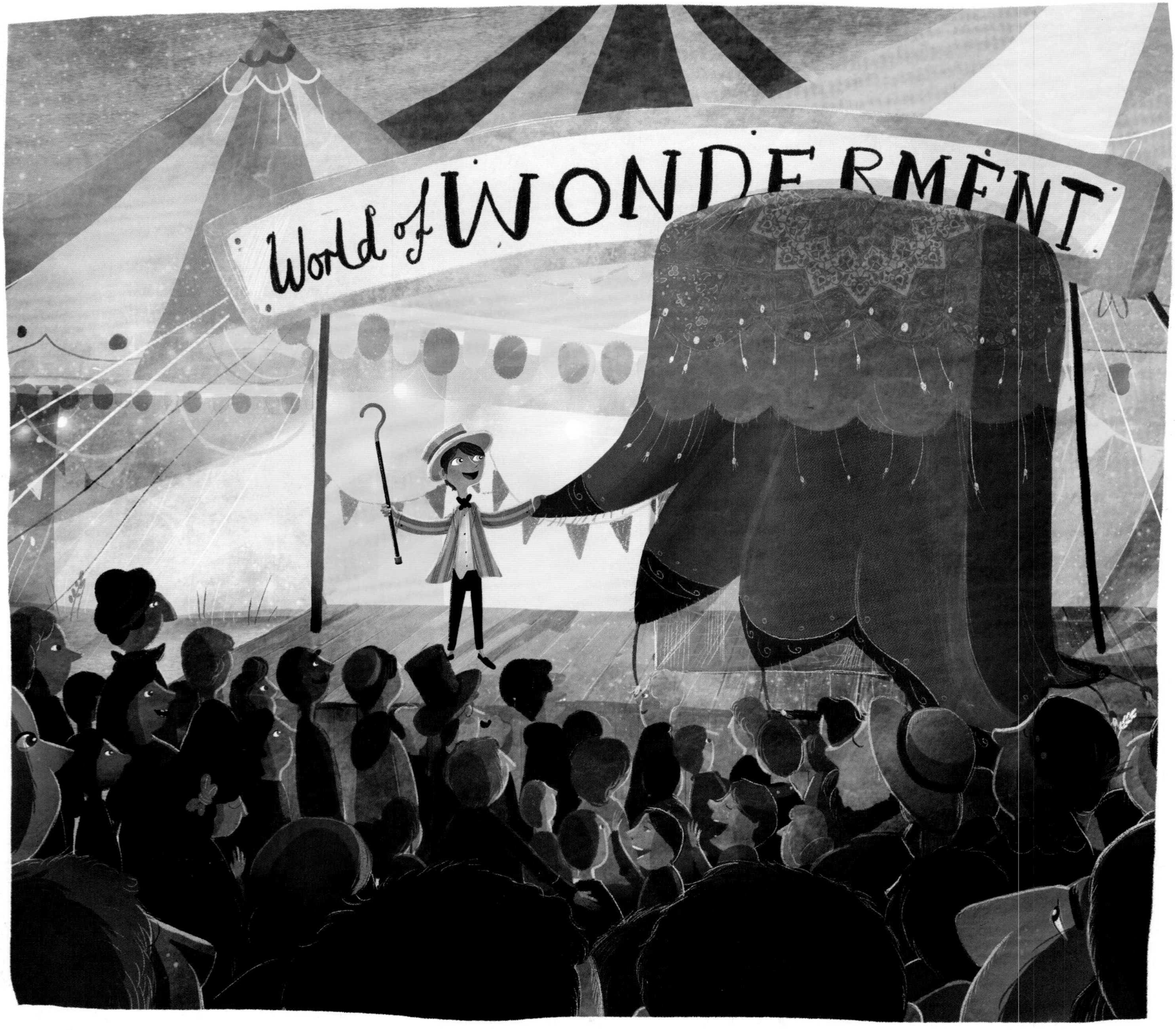
World of WONDERMENT

Sometimes we go looking for an adventure

only to discover exactly where we belong.

This world is full of remarkable people:

strangers who become friends,
and friends who become family,

surrounding us with a love that reaches from the sky to the sea.